To:

From:

Copyright © 2018 Marianne Richmond
Cover and internal design © 2018 by Sourcebooks, Inc.

Sourcebooks and the colophon are registered trademarks of Sourcebooks, Inc.

Published by Sourcebooks Jabberwocky, an imprint of Sourcebooks, Inc.
P.O. Box 4410, Naperville, Illinois 60567-4410
(630) 961-3900
Fax: (630) 961-2168
sourcebooks.com

Library of Congress Cataloging-in-Publication Data is on file with the publisher.

Source of Production: Worzalla, Stevens Point, WI, USA
Date of Production: July 2018
Run Number: 5012775

Printed and bound in the United States of America.
WOZ 10 9 8 7 6 5 4 3 2 1

You are my KiSS GOOD NiGHT

Written and illustrated by

Marianne Richmond

sourcebooks
jabberwocky

The moon is glowing up above.
GOOD NIGHT happy sun.
Stars turn on their twinkle lights.
It's bedtime, **little one.**

LOVE

MY DOG

Believe in yourself!

You are my JOY
in our every day through,
spending time with each other
and time apart, too.

You are my

THANKFUL

when we

think of the way

kindness and caring **brightened** our day.

You are my **BLESSING**

to grow you, my child,

my
proud
and my
patience,

my
wonder,
my
wild.

You are my **GIGGLE** when we laugh before bed,

sharing **stories** and **sillies** before resting your head.

You are my **PEACEFUL**
when we sing lullabies,
winding down **wiggles**
before closing your eyes.

You are my COZY

when we snuggle up tight,
trading **whispers** and **wishes**
before our good night.

with your **lovey** and **covers** pulled up to your nose.

You are my CALM
before drifting to sleep
when we ask happy dreams
to visit your sleep!

You are my **SLEEPY**
when I turn out the light.

My **HUG**
and my **LOVE,**

You are my KISS
GOOD NIGHT.